FJ
HA

‖‖‖‖‖‖‖‖‖ ⬧ **P9-BZF-160**

00101926
Hampstead Public Library

Unicorn School

Team Magic

Willow glanced up just as the Tricorn looked
around at them all, his eyes concentrating
particularly on the Year Ones. "I will *not* have
cheating in this school," he said firmly.
"We will find out who did this. If it is you, I urge
you to come forward before it is too late."

HAMPSTEAD PUBLIC LIBRARY
9 MARY E. CLARK DRIVE
HAMPSTEAD, NH 03841

WITHDRAWN

Linda Chapman lives in Leicestershire, England with her family and Bernese mountain dogs. She used to be a stage manager in the theater. When she is not writing, she spends her time looking after her young family, horse riding, and teaching drama.

Books by Linda Chapman

MY SECRET UNICORN series

UNICORN SCHOOL series

Unicorn School

Team Magic

Linda Chapman

Illustrated by Ann Kronheimer

SCHOLASTIC INC.

No part of this publication may be reproduced, stored in a retrieval system, or transmitted in any form or by any means, electronic, mechanical, photocopying, recording, or otherwise, without written permission of the publisher. For information regarding permission, write to Working Partners Limited, Stanley House, St. Chad's Place, London WC1X 9HH, United Kingdom.

ISBN 978-0-545-56589-9

Text copyright © 2009 by Working Partners Limited.
Illustrations copyright © 2009 by Ann Kronheimer.
Created by Working Partners Ltd.
All rights reserved. Published by Scholastic Inc.
SCHOLASTIC and associated logos are trademarks
and/or registered trademarks of Scholastic Inc.

12 11 10 9 8 7 6 5 4 3 2   13 14 15 16 17/0

Printed in the U.S.A.   40

This edition first printing, November 2012

To Suzanne Duxbury, for all the friendship, help, and support—and for going through everything with me!

gift 399 3/16

ARCADIA

Sea of Silence

Cloud
Stables

Rose Quartz
Cliffs

Beach

Moonlight
Meadows

The Telling
Tree

Assembly
Fields

UNICORN SCHOOL

High Winds Pass

Bramble Forest

Flying Heath

Charm Fields

N
W E
S

Contents

Delivering the Mail

The sun shone down on the glittering, pearly-white turrets of Unicorn School. It was early in the morning and most of the unicorns were still in their stables. Willow trotted across the courtyard, a mailbag swinging from her mouth. She felt very important. Usually all

the letters and packages that came
to Unicorn School were delivered
by the elves who worked there, but
that morning Willow had gotten up
early to mail a birthday card to her
dad and had been asked to help. It
was very exciting to be getting mail
because final exams were coming up

and all the parents were sending good-luck cards and little presents.

As Willow thought about the exams, a nervous shiver ran down her spine. She was in her first year at Unicorn School, which meant she had six exams to take, and she really wanted to do well. She'd been working very hard every evening for the past few weeks, reading through all her notes for the year. There was so much to remember!

She trotted into the tower that led to the Rainbow House stables. The unicorns who went to Unicorn School belonged to one of four houses, the others being Star House, Moon House, and Sun House.

Willow slept and ate with the seven other Year Ones who were also in Rainbow House. At the very top of the tower was a circular room with a door in the wall that led to the stables, which were set in the clouds.

Carrying the mailbag carefully, Willow went across the room and touched the door with her gold horn. The door swung open, revealing a corridor leading into a stable with eight stalls. Two of Willow's best friends, Sapphire and Storm, had their heads over their stall doors and were chatting.

"Hi, Willow!" Storm whinnied as she came down the corridor. He looked at the bag. "What do you have there?"

"Mwmph," Willow mumbled through a mouthful of bag. She put it down carefully. "Mail!" she said. "The elves are really busy with all the mail that's arriving, so they asked me if I would deliver it." She opened the bag and started to give out the packages and letters.

"There's a package for you, Sapphire." She passed a pink package to a very pretty unicorn with long eyelashes and a sweeping mane and tail. "And this is for you, Storm." She handed the tall unicorn a yellow package. "This green package is for Flint, the orange one for Starlight, and there are letters for Topaz and Ash." She trotted between the stalls, delivering the mail to the other Year Ones. They all whinnied gratefully.

"Is there anything for me?" asked a voice behind her.

Willow looked around. It was Troy, her other best friend. From his windswept mane and tail she guessed that he had been at early morning practice with the Flying Team.

"There's a letter for you," said Willow. "It looks like it's from your mom and dad," she added, seeing that it had a gold crown on the front. Troy's parents were the king and queen of Arcadia.

"Oh, good!" said Troy, pleased. "I

wrote to Mom asking her about
something important. I bet she's
replying to that."

"What were you asking about?"
Willow said curiously.

Troy shook his head. "I'm not telling."

"Why not?" asked Willow.

"Because it's something about you three," said Troy, looking at Storm and Sapphire.

"About us?" Storm said in surprise.

"What is it?" whinnied Sapphire.

"I said I'm not telling," replied Troy mysteriously. "Not yet. You'll just have to wait."

Willow and the others gave up asking him. They were all eager to see what was in their packages.

"Look!" whinnied Sapphire, opening hers with her horn. "Mom's sent me some ribbons for my mane to bring me luck!" She held up ten pale pink ribbons in her mouth.

"And I've got a cake to cheer me up while I'm working so hard!" said Storm, holding up a large frosted cake by the red ribbon that was wrapped around it. "We can all share it."

Willow pulled out her present. It was a necklace made of delicate white shells. "Oh, wow! I got a necklace!" She read the letter inside the package:

Dear Willow,
Your dad and I know how hard you have been working for your exams, and we are sending you this little present so that you know we're thinking about you.

*Just do your best and try hard and we'll
be very proud of you. Good luck! Love,
Mom and Dad XOXOXO*

A warm glow spread through
Willow. It was nice to know her
mom and dad were thinking about
her. She glanced at Troy. He didn't
look very happy.

"What does your letter say?" Willow nudged him gently with her horn. "Is it what you were expecting?"

"No," sighed Troy. "It doesn't say anything about what I asked. It's from my dad, not my mom, and it's just about the exams. Look." He pushed the letter toward Willow. She read it.

Dear Troy,

Your mother and I hope you are studying hard for your examinations. We don't need to remind you how important it is that you do well in all your subjects. As prince of Arcadia, you must set an example for others. We wish you all the

*best of luck and look forward to hearing
of your great achievements.*
 Your loving father

Willow thought about her own
letter and couldn't help feeling a bit
sorry for Troy. She knew that as
long as she tried her best on the
exams her parents would be proud
of her, no matter how she did, but
Troy's father made it sound like he
would be happy only if Troy did
really well.

"What am I going to do?" Troy
said. He looked at the letter again.
"What if I do badly in my exams,
Willow?"

"You won't," Willow said

encouragingly. "You're really good at everything, particularly flying."

"I suppose I am okay at most things. It's just history I find really hard," Troy said. "What if I fail?"

All the Year One unicorns took flying, charms, and transformation classes, and they also chose three of four other subjects: weather magic, healing, rose-quartz gazing, and history. Willow and Troy were the only two of the friends who took history.

"Oh, Troy. You won't fail," said Sapphire, listening in.

Troy stamped a hoof. "What do you know about it, Sapphire? You don't even take history. You have no idea how hard it is!"

Sapphire looked hurt.

"Troy! Don't get angry at Sapphire!" Storm protested. "It's not her fault you find history hard. Anyway, you chose to do it. You could have taken a different subject."

"No, I couldn't!" Troy exclaimed. "My parents wouldn't let me. They think that because I'm a prince it's really important that I know about the past and what has happened in Arcadia. I had to take history, but I'm no good at it!"

"Don't worry. I'll help you," Willow said quickly. "We can review together this week."

Troy gave her a grateful look.

"Thanks, Willow." He touched noses with Sapphire. "And I'm sorry I got angry at you, Sapphire. I'm a little nervous."

"That's all right," Sapphire whickered gently.

Troy sighed. "The sooner these exams are over the better."

Willow couldn't agree more!

Helping Troy

"Right, everyone. Next question."
Roswell, the pretty young
teacher who taught history, looked
around at the Year Ones who were
gathered in the classroom. "Who
won the War of the Great River?
Was it the ogres or the trolls?"

Willow put up her horn.

"Yes, Willow?"

"The ogres," Willow replied.

"Very good." Roswell nodded approvingly. "That's the fifth question you've answered correctly today. You've obviously been studying hard. Well done." Willow glowed with pride.

Roswell walked to the front of the room. "Now, let's have a look at what happened." She touched her horn to a large slab of shining white quartz. Its surface seemed to shimmer, and a moving picture appeared. It showed two armies, one made up of trolls and one of ogres. They were attacking each other with huge wooden clubs. As the

class watched, the ogres began to chase the trolls away. Then one of the trolls turned as if it was looking straight at them and roared, showing jagged yellow teeth. Willow shivered. She preferred it when Roswell showed them moments of history with animals and pixies and birds.

Roswell touched her horn to the quartz, and it went blank again. "Now, next question," she continued. "Which royal unicorn negotiated a truce between the pixies and the water sprites at the Rushing River twenty years ago?"

Several unicorns, including Willow, put up their horns, but Roswell was looking at Troy. "Troy!"

Willow felt Troy jump beside her. He'd been staring out the window. She was sure from the guilty look on his face that he'd been thinking about flying.

"You haven't answered any questions yet, Troy," Roswell said to him. "Can you tell me the answer to this one?"

"Um . . . it was . . . it w-w-was . . ." Troy stammered.

"Randulf the Twelfth," another student mumbled.

"Rudolph the Third!" Troy said, mishearing.

"No!" Roswell said angrily. "Rudolph the Third died a hundred years ago!" Some of the other unicorns giggled. "Really, Troy. You should have been able to answer that question. It was Randulf the Twelfth—your own uncle!"

"Uncle Ulf?" Troy looked astonished. "He negotiated a truce? That's amazing! It takes him an hour every dinnertime to decide between apples and carrots!"

The rest of the class giggled even louder. But Roswell didn't look amused. "This is not good enough, Troy. If you can't answer a simple question like the one I've just asked, how do you think you will ever pass the exam?"

Troy hung his head.

Roswell walked to the front and again touched her horn to the white quartz. This time the rock shimmered into a picture of a sparkling silver river rushing over a waterfall. A handsome, strong unicorn who looked like Troy stood beside it, and all along the riverbank tiny pixies and water sprites were dancing and swinging one another around by the hands.

Roswell continued asking questions

and showing scenes from Arcadia's history. Troy didn't say anything else for the rest of the lesson. Willow noticed that he was looking very down. "Are you okay?" she asked him when the lesson finished.

He shook his head. "What am I going to do, Willow? I'm never going to pass the exam. I'm lousy at history!"

"You're not lousy. You just need to go through your notes and start learning them," said Willow.

"But I don't have any notes!" Troy said despairingly. "Look!" He gave his history notebook to Willow. She put it on the floor and turned the pages. There were some notes at the beginning, but the later pages were filled with pictures of flying unicorns.

"Troy!" she said. "You haven't been listening at all in class, have you?"

"Not really," he said in a small voice.

Willow felt mad at him, but she

could see that wasn't going to help. "All right, look, you can borrow my notes. Meet me in the library at lunchtime, and you can start copying them. I'll explain anything you don't understand."

"Thanks," sighed Troy.

As soon as it was lunchtime, Willow went to the library. She was very hungry and really wanted her lunch, but helping Troy was more important. She decided she would grab some mouthfuls of grass in the meadows before afternoon classes started. Getting her history books out, she waited impatiently for Troy to arrive.

Fifteen minutes went by, twenty

minutes, twenty-five minutes . . .
Willow got increasingly worried.
Where was Troy? Why hadn't he
shown up? Suddenly, Troy came
trotting into the library. "Sorry I'm
late!" he gasped.

"Where have you been?"
demanded Willow. "I've been really
worried about you. I've been
waiting forever."

Troy looked a bit sheepish.
"Umm . . . I've . . . well, I've been
at flying practice."

Willow stared. "Flying practice!"

Troy nodded. "The Tricorn's asked the
Flying Team to do a show at the end
of the semester when the parents come,
so we have to practice every day."

Willow couldn't believe it. She'd
missed lunch and had been waiting
around in the library all because
Troy had been flying! "I thought
you wanted to pass your history
exam!" She began throwing books
into her bag. "I've been here all
lunchtime. You could have told me
you were going flying, and I'd have
done something else. Well, you can

forget about me helping you from now on!"

"Willow, wait!" Troy said quickly. "I just didn't think. Help me, please. I'm sorry you missed lunch. Look, stay here—just for one minute!" And before Willow could protest, he had cantered out of the library. She frowned. Where was he going?

A few minutes later, Troy came back with a bag of apples and carrots in his mouth. "I got these from the elves in the kitchens. I *am* really sorry I didn't come earlier. Please, will you still help me, Willow?"

He did look very sorry, and Willow felt her anger fade. "Okay," she said, biting into an apple.

"Thank you for the food. Let's review some history."

Troy nodded. "Yes, please."

Their review session wasn't a success, however. Willow tried to explain her notes, but every time she started talking, Troy stared into the distance and his eyes grew vacant.

"Are you listening to me, Troy?" Willow demanded when he had failed to answer a question for the third time.

"Mmm . . . what?" Troy blinked. "Oh, sorry. It's really hard. If only we knew what the exam questions were going to be—then we could just learn the answers to those questions."

"You know it doesn't work like that," Willow told him. "We have to learn everything."

"But there's just so much of it," said Troy. "I'm never going to be able to remember it all!"

"You will. You just have to keep trying," said Willow confidently.

A horn blew outside, signaling the end of lunchtime. Willow shut her books and sighed. "Come on. We can do some more later."

She left the library with Troy walking slowly behind her.

Chapter Three

Sapphire's Idea

When Willow and Troy arrived at the Charm Fields for their afternoon class, Sapphire and Storm were already waiting for them. "How did your studying go?" asked Storm when they met up.

"Not great," Troy sighed. "There's just so much to learn. I wish I knew what the exam questions were going to be, but I guess there's no chance of that. I could never get to see them—not when the elves have all the exam papers in big chests in the mail room."

"And even if you *could* see them, that would be cheating," Willow reminded him.

"Not really. I wouldn't be looking at the answers, just the questions," said Troy.

"It would still be cheating," said Willow. "Anyway, it's silly even thinking about it. There's no way to see the tests before the exam."

"I suppose you could always . . ." Sapphire broke off.

Troy looked at her curiously. "You could what?"

"It doesn't matter," said Sapphire, shaking her head.

Willow glanced at her, wondering what she'd been about to say. But just then Damaris, the charms teacher, flew down. "Okay, gather round, everyone!" she whinnied. "We have a lot of work to get through today!"

Willow moved forward with the other Year Ones. It seemed like there was a lot to do every day.

For the whole of charms class they practiced making good luck and good health charms, and then they had a transformation class. "Transformation" meant turning one thing into another. That day they were reviewing how to turn acorns into different types of food and flowers. Tor, the teacher, made them do it over and over again until they got it right.

By the end of the class, Willow's head was spinning. She'd been planning on studying before supper

but decided to go for a walk instead. She looked around for the others to see if they wanted to go with her, but Storm had already gone off with Flint to practice some weather magic, and Sapphire and Troy were nowhere to be seen, so Willow set off on her own.

Carefully, she picked her way down to the beach. She loved walking along the sparkling white sand and watching the crystal clear waves lapping against the shore. When she reached the beach, she breathed in deeply. The Rose Quartz Cliffs that towered above the white sands glimmered pink in the afternoon sunlight. It was very peaceful. *School's such hard work at the moment*, Willow thought as she began to walk along the beach. *I wish exams were over.*

After exams there was just one week of school left, with all sorts of fun activities planned: a picnic in the woods, a moonlight swim in the sea, a magic tournament in the Assembly Fields. The unicorns would then all get their exam results and go home the next day for summer vacation. Willow snorted. It was weird to imagine spending six weeks without Sapphire, Storm, and Troy. She was so used to seeing them every day! *I'll really miss them*, Willow realized. *I wish we could see each other during vacation*. . . .

Her thoughts changed when she noticed two unicorns standing near the cliffs a bit farther along the beach. They were deep in conversation, their backs to the sea, so it took a while before Willow realized it was Troy and Sapphire! What were they doing? She was about to whinny but stopped herself. It would be much more fun to sneak up on them instead and make them jump! She trotted over as quietly as she could.

Maybe they're about to do some rose-quartz gazing, Willow thought.

Unicorns could see anyone anywhere in Arcadia if they touched their horns to a rock of rose quartz and said the name of that person. Sapphire, who took rose-quartz gazing as one of her subjects, was very good at it.

As Willow got closer, she slowed to a walk and picked her way quietly over the rocks toward them.

"I *think* I could do it," Sapphire was saying to Troy. "I've been wondering about it all afternoon. It will be difficult because it's not like seeing a person, but I bet it's possible."

"Are you sure you don't mind?" asked Troy slowly.

"I'm sure," said Sapphire. "I know how worried you are and that it would really help you."

Willow frowned. What were they talking about?

"Okay, here goes," said Sapphire, stepping up to the cliff. She touched her horn to the rose quartz and whispered something under her breath that Willow couldn't quite hear. For a long moment, Sapphire concentrated hard, and then the rock shimmered and she gave a little gasp. "Look. It's working, Troy! A picture's coming."

Troy caught his breath. "I can see the papers in the chest! I can read them, Sapphire! Oh, wow!"

Willow crept closer. Her eyes widened as she saw the picture in the rose quartz—it was an exam paper lying inside a big wooden chest. An exam paper with the heading *Year One: History Exam.*

"What are you two doing?" she whinnied.

Sapphire and Troy both jumped about a foot into the air. They swung around, their faces full of guilt.

"Willow!" Troy exclaimed. "What are you doing here?"

Willow ignored the question. "You're cheating!" she cried. "You're using rose quartz to look at the exam papers!"

"Only the history one," said Troy defensively. "And I was just taking a quick look. I wanted to see the questions so I know what to review. I wasn't looking at the answer key."

"It's still cheating! You know it is!" Willow stared at him furiously and then swung around to Sapphire. "Sapphire! How could you use your magic for something like that?"

Sapphire looked very flustered.

"I—I just thought it would help Troy. I knew how worried he was, and I thought if I used my rose-quartz gazing skills to help him, it would be a nice thing to do. I—I didn't think it was that bad."

"Well, it is!" said Willow.

"Don't be angry with Sapphire," Troy said quickly.

"I'm not!" Willow exclaimed. And she wasn't really. She knew that, although it was wrong of Sapphire, she'd done it only because she was kind and didn't like seeing Troy unhappy. "I'm angry with *you*! I can't believe you'd let Sapphire use her magic so you could cheat."

"It was only a little look." Troy

tossed his head. "You're making a huge fuss about nothing. You're such a goody-goody!"

"I am not!" Willow said indignantly.

"I suppose you're going to tell the teachers now," Troy said, his expression half daring, half scared.

"No," said Willow, thinking that she wanted to but knowing that she couldn't get her friends into trouble like that.

Troy looked very relieved. "Thanks. Well, I'm going to go to the library to write down the questions before I forget them."

"But . . ." Willow began.

It was too late. Troy had already flown into the air and was galloping away.

Chapter Four

Keeping Secrets

Willow stared speechlessly after Troy. Beside her, Sapphire gave a distressed whinny. "I shouldn't have used the rose quartz to look. I feel awful now. I was only trying to help."

"I know," Willow said. She took a deep breath and felt her anger fade.

"It's not your fault, Sapphire. Not really. Troy shouldn't have let you use your magic to cheat."

"Don't tell anyone," begged Sapphire. "I know you said you wouldn't tell the teachers, but please don't say anything to anyone—not even Storm."

"We can't *not* tell Storm!" Willow protested. "He's our best friend."

"But I really don't want him to know," said Sapphire. "I feel so bad, and it makes Troy look bad, too." Willow hesitated.

"Please, Willow," Sapphire begged.

"Okay," Willow sighed, although she didn't like it. "I won't tell Storm."

When Willow and Sapphire got
back from the beach, they went
to have their supper. All meals
at Unicorn School were served
on four long tables in the
Moonlight Meadows. There were
holes for buckets in the tabletops,
and the unicorns were allowed to
eat as much as they wanted. That
evening the buckets were filled with
a warm bran mash, carrots, and

apples. Willow and Sapphire found
two places just as Troy arrived. He
came to stand beside them.

"Hi," he said.

"Hi," muttered Sapphire
awkwardly, but Willow turned her
back on him.

"Aren't you talking to me?" Troy
said.

"No," replied Willow.

Storm came trotting over. "Hi,

guys!" he whinnied as he joined them at the table. "What have you been doing?"

Sapphire, Willow, and Troy all spoke at the same time.

"N-nothing," Sapphire said.

"We've been at the beach," muttered Willow.

"I've been studying," said Troy.

Storm looked surprised. "Oh, right. So you've all been doing different things?"

"Yes," said Sapphire.

"No," said Troy.

"Sort of," said Willow.

Storm looked confused.

"What have you been doing, Storm?" Willow asked, to change the subject.

"I've been practicing flying." Storm

laughed. "I'm so useless at it I'm sure I'm going to fail the exam, so I went to talk to Atlas about it after class. He was really nice and gave me some exercises to practice. He also said he'll give me some extra teaching between now and the exams. I'm going to get up early and have a lesson every morning before school starts."

"That's really good," Sapphire said encouragingly.

Willow nodded. "Yes. It'll be hard work, but I bet you'll end up passing the exam." She shot a meaningful look at Troy. "It's much better than *cheating*." Troy looked uncomfortable.

"Of course it is!" said Storm.

"Cheating's terrible! I'd never do that."

"Me, neither," said Willow, still looking at Troy.

Troy cleared his throat. "I'm not feeling very hungry," he said. "I— I think I might skip supper tonight." And with that, he left the table and hurried away.

Storm looked surprised. "It's not like Troy to miss supper. Do you think he's all right? Maybe I should go after him."

"No, don't," Willow said, knowing that it was the talk of cheating that had made Troy leave the table. "He'll be fine."

"But he said he didn't feel hungry," Storm said.

"He'll be fine," repeated Willow.

Storm frowned at her. "What's going on? You're behaving really strangely."

"It's nothing," Willow muttered.

"Nothing at all," Sapphire added quickly. "Mmm." She dug her nose into her feed bucket. "This bran mash is delicious!"

"Yes, these apples are really yummy," said Willow.

Storm looked from one to the other. "There's something you're not telling me, isn't there?" When neither of them said anything, he looked upset. Burying his nose in his bucket, he didn't say another word for the rest of the meal.

Over the next week Willow only really talked to Sapphire. She was still very angry at Troy and wouldn't speak to him, and Storm was clearly upset with all three of them. Willow felt awful about not telling him what had happened, but she couldn't break her promise to Sapphire. She ended up spending most of her time in the library. It was good to get lots of study time in, but she did miss hanging out with Troy and Storm. It was always more fun when the four of them were doing things together.

At long last the exams started. They were being held in the Great Hall, where desks were lined up in rows. On each of them was a sheet of questions, turned over so the unicorns couldn't see what was on them until the exam started. There was also a sheet of sparkling white parchment to write the answers on and a silver inkwell full of purple ink. The unicorns could write by

dipping their horns into the ink. For most of their subjects, apart from history, the Year Ones had two exams—one in the Great Hall, where they had to write the answers down, and one outside, where they had to do magic to show what they had learned.

Although Willow was very nervous when the exams first started, she soon found that they weren't really that scary. She didn't know every answer on every exam, but she had a feeling she was doing well, and by the end of the week, she was almost beginning to enjoy herself. Even better, her friends seemed to be doing okay, too. Sapphire came out of the rose-quartz gazing exam looking very happy and Storm had practiced his flying so much that he managed to do almost everything Atlas asked.

The very last exam was history. Willow and Troy stood next to each other without speaking as they waited outside the Great Hall to be let in.

Roswell opened the big wooden doors. "You may all come in now," she said.

Troy glanced at Willow. "Good luck."

Willow hesitated. She couldn't bring herself to wish him luck, too. *It's not as if he needs it, anyway*, she told herself. *After all, he knows what the questions are going to be.* Avoiding his eyes, she hurried past him into the hall and found her desk. The exam was about to begin!

Chapter Five

Who's Been Cheating?

When all the unicorns were at their desks, Roswell tossed her head in the air, and a stream of silver stars flew out of her horn. When Willow had first seen a teacher do this at the start of an exam, she had been amazed, but now she was used to it. Each silver star landed on an exam paper. They twinkled for a moment and then vanished with a faint *pop*. The papers magically flipped over so the unicorns could read the questions, and the exam began!

Question 1: In what year did the Battle of the High Peaks start, and what role did the dragons play in it?

Easy, thought Willow, dipping her horn into the inkwell. She heard a faint gasp from beside her and looked at Troy. He was staring at the exam paper, his eyes wide.

Willow wondered what was wrong. But there was no time to think about it now. She knew they only had an hour to answer all the questions and she had to start writing.

For the rest of the hour Willow hardly looked up from her exam paper, but she was aware that, beside her, Troy was sighing and

shifting restlessly from side to side. He seemed to finish writing very early.

When the exam ended and Roswell collected all the papers, Troy cantered out of the hall, pushing past the other unicorns in his hurry to get out. Willow frowned. He didn't look very happy.

She made her way over to the Moonlight Meadows. Sapphire was waiting at the lunch table. She had finished her exams the day before. "How did it go?" she asked Willow eagerly. "I've been thinking about you and Troy all morning."

"It wasn't too bad. I could answer

most of the questions," Willow said.

"I guess Troy could answer them all," said Sapphire.

"Well, it was a bit odd." Willow told Sapphire about Troy's shocked look when he saw the questions and the way he had cantered off afterward.

"That's weird." Sapphire frowned. "I wonder why he did that?"

"I don't know. You'd think that he'd have been looking really happy. After all, he knew all the—" Just then Storm arrived and Willow quickly shut up.

Storm glanced at them curiously. "What are you two talking about?"

"Nothing," Willow muttered.

"Nothing you want *me* to hear, anyway," Storm huffed, looking hurt. "I was going to ask you how your exam went, but I guess there's no point. You probably won't tell me that, either!"

Willow felt awful. "Of course I'll

tell you about the exam," she began, but she broke off as an elf walked into the meadow and blew a horn.

"What's happening?" Sapphire said, surprised.

Willow didn't know. Her eyes widened as the Tricorn, a snow-white unicorn and the school's headmaster, came into the Moonlight Meadows. The Tricorn's horn was striped gold, silver, and bronze, and today there was an unusually serious expression on his noble face.

He stopped and looked around gravely. "Good afternoon, everyone. I am sorry to delay the start of your lunch, but I have some very disturbing news. It appears that last week someone used rose quartz to look into the chest containing the Year One history exam papers."

There was a gasp from the unicorns. Willow's stomach felt as if it had just been flooded with icy water. She glanced quickly at Sapphire.

"There is a spell placed on all the exam chests," the Tricorn continued. "It tells the elves when magic has been used by someone trying to cheat. When the elves opened the history chest this morning, they discovered that someone had been dishonest enough to try to use magic to look inside."

A chorus of whispers from the

listening unicorns ran around the
lunch tables.

"Who was it?"

"Who could it be?"

"Who would have done
something like that?"

Willow kept her eyes to the
ground. She didn't dare look up. She
was sure that if anyone saw her face
they would realize that she knew
the answer.

"This is obviously extremely
serious," the Tricorn said gravely.
"The other teachers and I can use
magic to discover exactly who used
rose quartz to try to cheat, but first
I want to give that unicorn a
chance to come forward. If no one

has confessed by tomorrow evening, we will begin work on the reveal spell and discover who it was."

Willow glanced up just as the Tricorn looked around at them all,

his eyes concentrating particularly on the Year Ones. "I will *not* have cheating in this school," he said firmly. "We will find out who did this. If it is you, I urge you to come forward before it is too late."

Turning around, the Tricorn walked quickly out of the meadow.

What Should
Sapphire Do?

As soon as the Tricorn had gone,
the unicorns at all four tables
started talking in whispers about
who could have cheated.

"I can't believe it," said Storm to
Willow and Sapphire, forgetting
about their earlier quarrel. "It's got
to be someone in your history class,

Willow. Who could it be?" Willow shrugged. Sapphire was looking as if she felt sick.

"I suppose it's got to be someone who also does rose-quartz gazing," continued Storm thoughtfully. "Who does both? Topaz, Starlight, and Moondust all do both subjects, don't they?"

"I . . . it doesn't have to be one of them," Sapphire said quickly. "Any unicorn can use rose quartz."

"Yes, but I bet you'd have to be really good at it to be able to look in the chest," said Storm. "Hmm, who could it be?"

Willow wasn't listening. She had caught sight of a figure in the

shadows of the nearby apple trees. "Troy!" she exclaimed.

"No, it couldn't be Troy," said Storm, thinking she was talking to him. "He's no good at rose-quartz gazing. And anyway, he wouldn't cheat."

"I'll be back in a minute," Willow said, setting off toward the trees.

She broke into a canter. Troy saw her coming and turned to go. "Troy!

Wait!" Willow whinnied. But he
didn't. He flew into the sky.

Willow chased after him as he shot
away toward the clouds. There was
no way she could keep up with
him—he was much better at flying
than she was—but she was
determined not to let him get away
completely. She gritted her teeth and
galloped after him as he twisted and
turned through the air and tried to

lose her.

"Troy! Come back!" she shouted angrily. "I want to talk to you!"

Willow knew that he couldn't go on flying forever, and at last he landed on the beach. Willow came down beside him. She was panting hard.

"What do you want?" Troy said defensively.

"Did you hear what the Tricorn said?"

"Yes." Troy looked uncomfortable.

"They know that someone has looked inside the chest. If they use magic to find out who it was, they'll see Sapphire!"

"It's not a big deal, Willow," Troy said quickly. "It's not like Sapphire does history. She can just say that she was rose-quartz gazing and . . . and looked into the chest by accident!"

Willow stared at him. "Oh, yes, they're *really* going to believe that!"

"They might," Troy said hopefully.

"They won't, Troy! They'll think she was trying to cheat for one of her other subjects, but the magic went wrong. You *have* to own up," Willow said. "You can't go ahead and get a good mark on your history exam while Sapphire gets into trouble!"

"I'm sure she won't get into trouble, and I know I'm not going to get a good mark," Troy said. "I'm sure I failed."

Willow was so surprised that for a

moment her anger left her. "What do you mean? How could you have failed?"

"I don't know. Maybe Sapphire's rose-quartz gazing magic wasn't good enough," said Troy. "But the questions we had to answer weren't the same ones I saw when I looked at the exam paper in the chest. None of

the questions I studied for came up."

He groaned. "I can't confess, Willow. It's going to be bad enough that I've failed the exam without being caught cheating, too. What would my father say if he was told that?"

Willow knew it was hard for him, but he *couldn't* let Sapphire take the blame. Despite what Troy said, she was sure everyone would think Sapphire had been trying to cheat. "You have to tell the Tricorn it was you," she told him.

Troy looked scared. "I can't." He shook his head. "No, I—I won't!"

Willow stamped a hoof furiously. "Then I don't want to be your friend anymore." She turned around and flew away.

"Willow!" Troy called after her.

But Willow didn't stop or turn around. *Maybe I should tell the Tricorn the truth*, she thought. But the idea made her feel cold inside. She hated the idea of telling on Troy.

Feeling too worried to eat, she didn't go back to the lunch table but headed to the cloud stables. Sapphire was there with Storm. He was looking very concerned. "If you're feeling ill, Sapphire, you should tell one of the teachers," he was saying as Willow walked into the stable. "Please let me go and get one of them."

Sapphire shook her head. "No, please don't."

Storm saw Willow. "Willow, where did you go? Sapphire says she's feeling really sick, but she won't let me tell a teacher."

Willow and Sapphire looked at each other.

"Tell her that she should let us get someone," Storm said.

"No," Sapphire said quickly.

"Let's not," said Willow.

"But why?" demanded Storm. When neither of them said anything, he looked angry. "Oh, this is another of your little secrets, isn't it?" He stormed out of the stable, pushing past Willow and cantering down the corridor.

"Oh, Willow!" Sapphire burst out. "This is dreadful. I don't know what to do. The Tricorn's going to find out that I was the one who looked in the chest."

"You're going to have to go and tell him the truth—tell him that you did it for Troy," said Willow.

Sapphire looked horrified. "I can't do that! Troy will get into real trouble."

"But if you don't, they might think you were trying to cheat for yourself and that the magic just went wrong," said Willow. "It *is* Troy's fault."

Sapphire looked awful. "I can't do

it. I can't!" Tears welled in her eyes.

Willow nuzzled her. If only
Sapphire had never suggested
looking in the rose quartz. If only
Troy had said no when she *had*
suggested it! Now everything had
gone wrong. She wasn't friends with
Troy anymore, and Storm was angry
with her, and Sapphire was going to

get into lots of trouble.

"I wish none of this had ever happened," Sapphire said unhappily.

"So do I," sighed Willow.

"I do, too."

They turned around. Storm had come back without them realizing it. "Why won't you tell me what's going on?" he asked them. "I thought we weren't supposed to keep secrets from each other."

"We're not supposed to." Willow looked at Sapphire. "Please tell him."

Sapphire hesitated and then nodded. "I'm sorry, Storm. Willow's been wanting to tell you what's been going on, but I said we couldn't because I felt really awful and it makes Troy look bad."

"Why?" said Storm.

"Listen, and I'll tell you every-thing," Sapphire said. And she did.

Storm listened in astonishment. "I can't believe Troy cheated like that! But I'm sure he's going to confess now that he knows the Tricorn's found out about it."

Willow shook her head. "He won't."

Storm looked at Sapphire. "Then you have to tell the Tricorn what happened," he said firmly. "They'll think you were trying to cheat. You can't take the blame, and it's not fair of Troy to expect you to. If you won't tell the Tricorn, then I will.

I'll go find him right now."

Sapphire hesitated and looked at Willow.

"Storm's right," Willow said. "You should tell the Tricorn the truth."

Sapphire took a deep breath. "Okay. I don't want to, but I will."

"It's the right thing to do," Storm said, nuzzling her. "Do you want us to come with you?"

Sapphire shook her head.

"Good luck," Willow told her.

Sapphire gulped. "Thanks. I think I'm going to need it!"

Chapter Seven

Telling the Truth

Willow and Storm waited anxiously for Sapphire to come back. After a little while they heard the door opening.

"How did it—?" Willow broke off. It wasn't Sapphire. It was Troy. "Oh," she said. "It's you." Troy headed for his stall.

"Willow and Sapphire have told me what happened," Storm said, stepping out in front of him.

Troy stopped. "They told you!"

Storm nodded. "I can't believe it, Troy. You tried to cheat, and now you won't own up to it. That's awful."

"It's all right for you, Storm. Your father isn't the king of Arcadia," Troy protested.

"That doesn't make any difference!" Storm exclaimed. "You shouldn't have done it. I don't think I want to be friends with you anymore. How can you let Sapphire take the blame?"

"I told you—I don't think she'll have to," Troy said desperately. "The Tricorn knows she doesn't take history."

"But he'll still think she was trying to cheat," Storm said.

"You should have confessed," said Willow. "It's too late now, anyway. Sapphire's gone to tell the Tricorn what really happened."

Troy stared at her in horror. "She hasn't!"

"She has," said Storm. "She didn't want to, but I told her that if she didn't, I would."

The door opened. This time it *was* Sapphire. She looked very upset, and big tears were rolling down her nose.

"Sapphire! What happened?" Willow asked. "What did the Tricorn say?"

"He said that he couldn't tolerate cheating and that I might be sent home from school and not be allowed to come back." A loud sob escaped Sapphire.

"What?" Storm burst out. "But he must have realized you weren't cheating—you don't even take history."

"I—I didn't tell the truth," Sapphire said. "I couldn't." She glanced at Troy. "When I told the Tricorn I was the one who looked into the chest, he asked why I had looked at the history exam. I just couldn't get Troy into so much trouble, so I said my magic went wrong—that I was trying to look at the charms exam and had made a mistake."

"So the Tricorn thinks you really *were* trying to cheat," Willow said in dismay.

"Yes," Sapphire whispered.

Willow swung around to Troy.

"Troy! You can't let Sapphire take the blame! You . . ."

But Troy was already walking toward Sapphire. "Don't worry, Sapphire," he said, interrupting Willow. "You've been a really good friend. It was very brave of you not to tell the Tricorn the truth. You tried to stop me from getting into trouble, but I can't let you be punished. I honestly didn't think you would be, but if the Tricorn really does think you were cheating, then I'll go and see him right away."

"But Troy! You'll be sent home!" protested Sapphire.

"I deserve to be." Troy's voice shook. "This is all my fault."

Willow breathed out. "Oh, Troy."

He swallowed. "I've been really stupid. I'm not surprised you don't want to be my friends. I wouldn't want to be my friend, either."

Willow hurried forward and touched him with her nose. "You know, I actually *do* want to be friends with you now."

"Me, too!" Storm joined them. "You're being really brave."

Sapphire nodded.

Troy looked around at them all. "Will you still be friends with me even if I'm sent home?" They all nodded.

"And we'll come with you to see the Tricorn," said Sapphire. "Whatever he says, we'll be with you."

Troy managed a small smile. "Thank you," he said.

The Tricorn's study was just beside the Great Hall. Troy knocked on the door with his horn.

"Come in," the Tricorn called.

Troy pushed open the door and all four unicorns trotted in.

The Tricorn was standing behind his big wooden desk. "Hello," he said. "What can I do for you?"

"I've got something to tell you, Tricorn." Troy swallowed nervously. "I . . . it . . . well, Sapphire wasn't cheating." The words suddenly rushed out of him. "She did use her magic to look inside the history

chest, but it was to help me. I was
the one who was cheating. Punish
me, but please, please, don't send
Sapphire home. She didn't look so
she could cheat!"

"I know." The Tricorn's deep voice
was very serious.

"You know?" Troy stared.

"Someone who is as good at rose-quartz gazing as Sapphire would never make such a mistake as looking into the wrong chest," said the Tricorn. "I knew she wasn't telling me the truth." He looked at Sapphire. "I hope you have learned a lesson from this, Sapphire. You must never again use your magic to help someone cheat."

Sapphire bit her lip. "I'm sorry. I promise I'll *never* do it again."

"Then we will say no more about it," said the Tricorn in a more kindly voice. He looked at Troy. "And now for you."

"I know you're going to send me

home." Troy hung his head. "But I deserve it."

"I'm not going to send you home, Troy," the Tricorn said.

Troy looked up in surprise. "What?"

"You have behaved very badly, but in the end, when it looked like your friend was going to be in trouble, you came forward and told the truth. Because of that I am going to give you a second chance. You may stay here at Unicorn School, although you will have to retake your history exam in a week's time."

"That's the day before vacation!" said Troy.

"Yes," the Tricorn replied. "I am

afraid if you are going to do the work needed to pass you will have to miss out on many of the end-of-year activities."

"That's okay!" Troy gasped. "I don't care. I'll work and work and work. I just want to pass the exam and do it without cheating."

"I'll help you," Willow promised. "We can use my notes—for real this time!"

"We'll help, too," Storm said, looking at Sapphire, who nodded.

"We might not take history ourselves, but we can help by testing you," she said.

"Thank you!" Troy told them gratefully. He looked at the Tricorn.

"And thank you for giving me another chance."

"I believe that courage should be rewarded, and it must have taken a great deal of it for you to come here and confess," the Tricorn said. "If you pass the exam, nothing more will be said about this whole incident, and I will not mention it to your parents." Troy looked very relieved.

"You may go now," the Tricorn told him. "Work hard, Troy."

"I will," Troy promised seriously. "And I'll never cheat ever again." He turned to go and then stopped, frowning. "Please, may I just ask you one thing?"

The Tricorn nodded. "Of course."

"Well, the history exam paper I saw—when Sapphire used the rose quartz—it was different from the one in the chest. Why was that?"

The Tricorn gave a small laugh. "That was because all of the chests

have a deception charm on them as well as a cheating spell. Not only do the elves know when someone has been looking at the paper dishonestly, but the paper itself shows the wrong questions—so the unicorn who is cheating does not benefit." He leaned forward, suddenly serious. "You don't think you are the first unicorn to have thought of using rose quartz to cheat, Troy? Magic can be very tempting at times. Just remember to use it only for good in the future." His expression softened. "Now go."

As soon as the door was shut behind them, Troy breathed a huge sigh of relief. "Phew! I don't have to go home! Will you all help me study for the exam like you said?"

"Of course!" Willow, Sapphire, and Storm chorused.

Troy looked determined. "I'm going to work so hard. I'm going to pass this exam. I have to!"

The End of the Semester!

"Okay, Troy. Who were the two leaders in the Battle of the Dragons?" Willow looked at Troy.

"Fangtooth and Gracken," Troy replied promptly.

"Which unicorn first discovered the magic of rose-quartz gazing?" Sapphire asked.

"Queen Starbright the Second," answered Troy.

"And who was the fastest unicorn ever?" questioned Storm.

Troy tossed his mane. "That's easy—Silverhoof. He won every race there ever was while he was at school, and he holds the record for being the fastest unicorn to fly around Misty Mountain and the fastest unicorn to fly from the High Winds Pass to the palace."

Willow felt a rush of relief. It was five days since Troy had confessed to the Tricorn that he had cheated, and since then he had been working really hard. First, he had copied out all his missing history notes, and then he had tried to learn everything so he could remember it for the exam. Willow, Storm, and Sapphire had spent every minute they could testing him, and it finally looked as if all the hard work was beginning to pay off. Every question they had asked that day, Troy had answered correctly!

"You're doing so well," Willow told him.

"Thanks to all of you," Troy said gratefully. "I'd never have been able to learn so much without your help. You've been great friends. You've missed all the fun end-of-semester stuff to help me."

"You've missed out on everything, too," Storm told him. "You even pulled out of the Flying Team display, and I know you really wanted to do that."

"I couldn't have gone to all the practices *and* studied as much as I needed to," Troy said.

"I can't believe the exam is tomorrow," said Storm.

Troy looked anxious. "Neither can I."

"You'll be okay," Sapphire reassured him.

Troy gulped. "I hope you're right," he said.

The next morning, Troy went nervously into the Great Hall to take his exam. All the other exams were over, and he was the only unicorn in there. As Roswell shut the door, Willow thought how lonely Troy looked standing behind a desk in the huge room, all on his own.

"I hope he gets the answers right," she said anxiously to Sapphire and Storm.

Storm nodded. "I'm more nervous about Troy taking this exam than I am about getting my own test results this afternoon." Willow knew just how Storm felt!

The hour seemed to take forever to go by. Storm paced up and down, Willow fidgeted anxiously, and Sapphire kept sighing in a worried way. At long last it was over. The door opened and Troy came trotting out. His ears were pricked and his eyes were bright.

"Well?" Willow demanded.

"It was actually okay!" Troy burst out. "There were a few questions that I didn't know, but all the others were fine!"

"Phew!" Sapphire said, tossing her mane with relief.

"That's wonderful!" said Storm.

"I'm just glad it's over," said Troy. "Come on, let's get out of here and go outside!" They cantered happily out to the meadows. The sun was shining, and the other unicorns in the school were all out enjoying themselves.

"Have you heard the news?" Oriel, a Year Three unicorn, came racing over to them. "The Tricorn has just announced that there'll be a big party in the Assembly Fields after the exam results this afternoon. There's going to be a feast and music, and the teachers are going to do a magic show!"

"Cool!" Troy exclaimed.

Willow grinned at him. "Looks like we haven't missed all the fun stuff, after all!"

As soon as lunch was over, the unicorns went to the Great Hall to get their exam results. Each desk had a name tag and a blank piece of paper on it. Willow's heart thudded as she found the desk with her name on. This was it—the moment they would find out how they had done. She glanced at Troy standing at the desk beside her.

"Good luck," he whispered.

"You, too," replied Willow.

The Tricorn was waiting at the

front of the hall. The chief elf stood
beside him. As the last few unicorns
found their desks, the Tricorn
stamped his front left hoof on the
ground. Absolute silence fell.

"It is now time for you to discover

the results of your examinations," the Tricorn told the waiting unicorns. "When the shell is blown, you must touch your horn to the piece of paper in front of you. Count to three, and when you raise your heads, the paper will reveal your results."

The chief elf raised the shell to his lips. The Tricorn nodded, and a long note sounded. Taking a deep breath, Willow touched her horn to the paper. A small purple spark burst from the end of it. *One, two, three,* Willow counted, then raised her head. Purple writing had appeared.

Willow—Year One
Examination Results
Charms . . . A *(excellent)*
Flying . . . B *(good)*
Transformation . . . B *(good)*
Weather Magic . . . A *(excellent)*
Healing . . . B *(good)*
History . . . A *(excellent)*

Willow felt a *whoosh* of delight. She had passed all her exams with a good or excellent grade in every one! How amazing was that?

She swung around to find her friends. As she did so, the Tricorn's voice boomed out, "When you have read your exam results, you may leave the hall."

The unicorns immediately raced around the hall, all asking the same questions of their friends. "What did you get? What grades?"

"Well?" Willow demanded as she, Storm, Sapphire, and Troy met up. They were all smiling.

"I got A's in transformation and weather magic and B's in everything else, apart from flying, which I got a C in!" Storm burst out. "But at least I passed it!"

"I got A's in healing, weather magic, and rose-quartz gazing, B's in charms and flying, and a C in transformation," said Sapphire, beaming.

Willow babbled out her own results, and then they all looked at Troy.

"I got A's in flying, healing, weather magic, and charms," he said slowly, "and a B in transformation. And in history . . ." He paused.

"Yes?" Willow demanded, hardly daring to breathe.

"I got a B!" Troy exclaimed. Willow, Sapphire, and Storm whinnied in delight.

"You passed!" exclaimed Storm.

"You didn't just pass, you got a B!" said Sapphire.

"That's great, Troy!" Willow said.

Troy grinned at them all. "I couldn't have done it without your help. Thank you!" Willow didn't think she'd ever felt happier.

Oriel came over. "Are you guys

coming to the party in the Assembly
Fields?" he asked.

Willow bucked joyfully. "You bet!"
she said.

The party was great fun. There was
a feast of fresh shamrock and all
sorts of games and things to do—
apple bobbing, a grab bag, pin the
tail on the paper unicorn, musical

statues, flying races, and guess the pixie's name. After the feast the teachers put on a magic show. Atlas and Fabian, the flying teachers, had everyone gasping as they flew four loop-the-loops one after the other, and on the final loop shot silver stars out of their horns. Tor turned a chair into a giant frosted cake and made strings of mini unicorns to decorate the trees. Elderflower, the weather magic teacher, made a glass of water change ten different colors, first one after the other and then all together so the glass had multicolored layers and looked like a rainbow. And the Tricorn demonstrated some of the most difficult unicorn magic by making himself invisible and reappearing behind trees and bushes in a silver flash. It was a wonderful display, and at the end everyone cheered.

"This is just the best day ever!" said Willow happily.

As she spoke, an elf came over to Troy and gave him a piece of paper. "It's a message from my parents," Troy said, looking at the royal crown on the front. He opened it and read what it said out loud. "Oh, wow! Listen to this:

Dear Troy,
Your mother and I have just heard
from the Tricorn about your excellent

exam results. We are delighted with how well you have done in your first year. Your mother tells me that in your last letter you asked if your friends Willow, Sapphire, and Storm could come to stay with us at the palace for a week during vacation. We would be delighted to have them come to visit."

Willow, Storm, and Sapphire gasped. Troy grinned at them. "So, will you come to the palace?" he asked eagerly.

"Oh, yes!" they all whinnied.

Willow's mind raced: a trip to the palace and a chance to spend a whole week of the vacation with

Storm and Sapphire and Troy. It sounded great!

"We'll be able to do lots of things," Troy went on. "There are sugar-coated apples growing on the trees, magic birds who sing whatever songs you want to hear, butterflies who perch on your back, and lots of secret passages in the castle to explore and play hide-and-seek in."

"Wow!" said Sapphire.

"It'll be amazing," said Willow.

"And best of all, we'll be together," Storm added happily.

Willow grinned. "No, what's really best of all is that after such a cool summer vacation we'll all be coming back here for another year!"

"And this time we'll be in Year Two," Sapphire pointed out.

"I wonder what that will be like," said Troy.

"One thing's for sure," said Willow, tossing her mane excitedly. "It's going to be fun!"